I0624932

Peter Elph

A Short Story

by

Dani Haviland

USA Today Bestselling Author

Cover by Michele Hauf

Book Description

Trouble and three bullets weren't all the gambler found in 1886 Tombstone. The woman he lost years before was there —
with a forty-
pound surprise.

Dedication

This book is dedicated to my mother, Lou Woodward. Over fifty years ago, she composed a short story called Peter Elf. She read it to us every Christmas Eve, a very important part of our Christmas tradition. I don't know what happened to her pen and notebook paper story of the little toy elf that Santa helped to the top of the Christmas tree, but her love and devotion to the written word still remains with me. Love ya, Mom. Rest in Peace.

Chapter 1

December 20, 1886
Tombstone, Arizona Territory

"Get out of there!" the crotchety storekeeper hollered.

"But I can sweep the floors and kill all the spiders. I can even bring my cat with me next time and she'll kill any mice that happen to sneak in the storeroom," Petey said, his eyes tearing in desperation as he begged.

"I don't have any work for you. Asides, even if you did work just for some penny candy, who says you wouldn't be stealing other goods? These dried figs are worth a lot more than your skinny little hide. Now, get outta here!" he screeched, swinging his cane at the five-year-old. "Damned orphans anyhow."

Petey wiped his nose with the sleeve of his patched and tattered thrice handed down jacket and sniffed back his frustration. He was young, but maybe he could get a job as a spittoon cleaner.

"Watch it!" a trail-worn cowboy on horseback hollered as he rushed across the dusty road to The Bird Cage Theater.

Petey scrambled to a hitching post and held on tight, seeking protection from the riders who always seemed to be in a hurry.

"Hey, kid. Can you tell me where the livery stable is?"

Looking up, Petey saw another new face. He didn't look like a miner or rancher, though. He was young, wearing a fancy dark coat and colorful vest, but his hat looked like he'd been wearing it for years. "It's right around the corner, Sir. It's called the O.K. Corral. If you'd like, I can show you the way for a penny."

"No offense, kid, but I think I can find my way," the dark-haired man said, then watched as hope slipped off the child's face. It was then he noticed the condition of the boy's clothes and his rag-tied feet. It was doubtful that there had ever been shoes under the scrap leather. "On second thought, why don't you show me? It's getting late and I might have a job for you once we get there."

"Yes, Sir!" Petey said, his face aglow. "I'm a real good worker. My mama tells me so all the time."

"And your pa? What does he have to say about it?" the stranger asked.

Petey's frown returned. "I don't have one, Sir," he said. "That's why I need a job: to help Mama. We have a real clean boarding house if you're looking for a place to stay. She gives a discount if you pay in advance or want more than one night, too."

"Sounds like you're quite the salesman, kid. So, is this the livery stable?"

"Yes, Sir. Do you want me to carry your bags for you?"

"Leave the man alone, Petey," a leather-aproned man said.

"Oh, I'm helping him, Mr. Joshua. Really, I am. Just ask him," Petey said, taking a cautious step back in case the blacksmith and stable operator decided to shove him out of the way. Again.

"Mr. Joshua?" the rider asked.

The big man nodded.

"I'm Peter Wagner. I'll only be staying a day or two. I'd like the boy to stay with my mare. Not to take care of her, but to keep her company. She's due to foal in a week or two and is a little skittish. I sing to her when I'm on the trail, and it seems to soothe her. If you don't mind," Peter reached in his vest pocket and pulled out a coin, "Would you feed both of them? Not the sour stuff for the horse, either. I'm sure you can scare up a bowl of stew or a bite of meat and bread for the boy. He looks like he's missed a meal or two lately. I want him to stay warm, too, so make sure he has a clean blanket. I might not be back until noon tomorrow."

"But..." Petey began, then quickly pursed his lips. "But," he began anew, "what do I do if she starts to foal? Where will you be?"

"If something goes amiss, I'll be in the saloon where I first saw you. I'm sure Mr. Joshua will get word to your mama that you have a job tonight." Peter looked over at the blacksmith, his eyes squinted menacingly. "Won't you?"

Mr. Joshua wrinkled his face as he snorted, then spat a wad of phlegm a hand's width away from Petey's feet. "Yeah, sure," he said, then chuckled as the boy flinched.

"On second thought," the stranger said, picking up his saddlebags, "maybe I'll see if there's another livery stable around…"

"No…no, Sir," Mr. Joshua stammered, grabbing a clean blanket from the shelf and handing it to Petey. "I meant no disrespect. It's just these kids around here, always looking for a handout. They're worse than rats!"

"Mr. Joshua, rats come in all configurations. This fine young lad asked for a job, and I gave him one. Seeing as I've hired both of you for different tasks, I'd say you were equals. Let's see who's more responsible, shall we?"

"Yes, Sir," Mr. Joshua said, then looked askance at Petey and sneered. "Venison stew good enough for ya, kid?"

"And some bread, too," Peter added.

He turned to the boy and winked. "The mare's name is Sweet Mary. Any song you know will work. There's a new one out, 'My Darling Clementine,' that she seems to like most."

"I've heard that one!" Petey exclaimed.

"Well, even if you don't know the words, make up some new ones. It's the tune that settles her."

"Yes, Sir. And thank you for trusting me. I'll see you tomorrow."

Peter grinned at the cute boy who reminded him of himself when he was that age: determined to help Mama and with a cowlick that couldn't be tamed. He looked at Joshua. "And don't forget to tell his mother where he is."

"Yes, Sir," Joshua replied, then turned away, determined that he wouldn't set foot near that woman's house. Banker Wilson would ruin anyone who even looked like they were helping Widow Elph.

***

Peter walked in the saloon and looked around, then sat down at the bar. "Whiskey," he said, then laid down a coin.

Branson the bartender brought out a shot glass and poured out a splash. Peter looked at the scant amount, then up at the man with the oversized mustache. "I think there's something wrong with your sight," he said coolly. "Look again. You missed."

Glancing up to make sure he wasn't being watched, Branson nodded to Peter and poured amber liquid to the rim. He bent forward and whispered, "The boss docks us if we're too generous with the spirits," then looked over at the potbellied man with the wide-brimmed Stetson.

Peter wrapped his hand around the glass so the contents couldn't be seen, then threw back the shot, gasping and coughing at the harshness of the drink. "I think one will be enough of that stuff." He cut his eyes over to the table where the boss was sitting, then looked back at the bartender. "I take it that he spends a lot of time in here."

"Yeah. If he was paying, he'd be his own best customer. Banker Wilson owns the bank, but does most of his business here, if you know what I mean."

Just then, a ruckus began at the table. Peter turned at the unmistakable click of a gun being cocked.

"Just hand over the deed, Joe," Banker Wilson said, his Colt pointed at the thin-faced farmer. "You never made a lick of money off that piece of land anyhow. Pack up the missus, goats, and kids and see if you can make a go of it in California. Word is, they're looking for folks like you."

Joe looked over at the bartender, then Peter, then everyone else in the room, hoping for intervention.

Everyone but Peter turned away. Peter answered the visual plea with a shrug. He'd been the new man in town enough times to know that you never got involved, especially when a rich man was holding a gun.

"I still say the cards were stacked," Joe said, then stood up and slapped his hand on the table, the deed to his property underneath it.

"Are you calling me a cheat?" the banker asked, standing up to face his accuser, his gun still pointed at him.

"No," Joe said, his voice low as he pushed the deed closer. "I guess not." He took a deep breath and let it out. "Just give me and the wife a day or two to gather everything up. We'll be out by Sunday."

"Make it Saturday," the banker said, palming the deed towards him.

"Yes, Sir," Joe mumbled, then shuffle-footed out the door.

"Looks like you have an empty seat," Peter said, walking over to the table. "Faro?"

"Yeah on both counts. You in?" The banker reached out his hand. "Name's Lee Wilson. I own this place, the bank, and just about everything else in this town."

"That's admirable," Peter said, shaking the man's hand heartily, curious to see if hidden cards would slip out with the action. "And from what I've seen so far, it's a mighty nice place. I might want to settle here. Got any nice ranches for sale?" he asked, adding a wink at the deed still lying on the table.

"Got lots of 'em," Wilson said. "Let's see how the night goes. Maybe you'll get lucky."

Peter spent the first few hours playing conservatively, watching the banker's eyes for the little signals that meant he was dealing from the bottom of the deck.

"Anyone here ever heard of the five-card draw version of poker? All fifty-two cards in the deck are used, not just the twenty."

"Yeah, I heard of it," Wilson said, readjusting his suspenders, winking to his wingman.

"He's pretty good at it," his cohort said. "We've all played it a time or two. How about we play 'til sunup?"

"I never heard of putting an end time to a card game," Peter said, "but I'm game for anything new."

The hours passed without excitement. Peter continued to play cautiously, but became more ambitious — and won larger sums — as morning approached.

"Are you some kind of hustler?" Wilson

growled when Peter raked in the last, and largest, pot.

"No, Sir. I'm just lucky. You've been the dealer all night, so there's no way I could have cheated."

"I think you're hiding cards. Take off that jacket and let my man check it out."

"I will if you will," Peter said. "Only I want someone else to check them, not your 'man.'"

Peter looked around the room and realized that there wasn't a neutral party. Rather than declare it, he stood up and started to take off his jacket.

"Watch it! He's drawing on me!" Wilson shouted.

Pop! Pop! Pop!

The banker quickly fired three rounds. His hands still in his sleeves, Peter slumped forward; cards and chips scattering as he crashed face first onto the table.

"Crap, Boss," the bartender said, rushing to Peter's side. He checked the coat and verified what he suspected. "He's unarmed. You blew it."

"Looks to me like he was drawing on me, right boys?" Wilson said, a worried sweat beading on his forehead. "Take him out of here before one of the Earps hears about it."

"I got this," the bartender said. He stood behind Peter and hoisted him under the arms, dragging what he thought was a corpse towards the door.

"Oh..." Peter groaned as his feet bumped the threshold.

"See!" Wilson crowed victoriously as he stood up. "He's still alive. Now, get him on his horse and send both of them away. We don't need riff-raff like him in this town anyhow."

***

Knock! Knock! Knock!

Mary Elph answered the desperate pounding on the door. "Oh, my Lord!" she screeched when she saw the situation. "Bring him in. Is he still alive?"

The bartender lifted the hat off Peter's face and saw the man's eyes squint tight in pain at the light of her lantern. "Yeah.

Barely. Your son said you could fix up people and critters pretty good. Banker Wilson shot him in cold blood. Says he drew first, but all of us that was there saw it. He was just trying to take his coat off and didn't even have a gun."

"Yeah," Petey said. "He's the guy who paid me to sing to his horse and keep her company while he was at The Birdcage. Is he gonna be okay, Ma?"

"We'll see. Bring him in the parlor, would you? Petey, go get all the lanterns you can find. It's so dark tonight, I can't tell anything," she said, as she cleared the way.

"By the way, I'm Branson, Mrs. Elph. Sorry no one's come to welcome you to town. Mr. Wilson put the word out that he wanted this place, and the only way to get it was if you couldn't make a go of it as a boarding house."

"Yeah, well he'd have to do more than that to make me give up this place. If he keeps collecting deeds like colorful ribbons, he's going to find himself with a bullet in the back." Mary cleared her throat and clutched her dressing gown closer. "Sorry. That was crude. I'm not suggesting I'd do anything like that…"

"Don't concern yourself," Branson said. "He gets at least one death threat a day. Oh, and I brought this for you. The old doc we had always insisted on pouring it over his sharps before cutting into a body. I figured you might need a bit to pour down his gullet to dull the pain, too."

"I don't want to force liquids if he's unconscious," Mary said. "Petey! What's taking you so long?"

"My horse," Peter mumbled. "Is she all right?"

Petey handed his mother the two lanterns, then leaned in close to answer his question. "Yes, Sir. I took good care of her. She was a little spooked coming here to my house, you smelling like blood and all. But I remembered to sing Clementine to her and she settled right down."

Peter's hand settled on Petey's then slipped down, a raspy gasp escaping.

"Help me get him on the table,

Branson. Petey, you light the lanterns and bring me my doctorin' kit."

Goosebumps raised as Mary cleaned his chest swiping in and around the wounds with whiskey and a wad of combed cotton. Although unconscious, Peter arched his back in pained reflex, but the two impromptu nurses were able to hold him down while Mary extracted the slugs.

"He was lucky," Mary said. She dipped her hands in the porcelain bowl of water and whiskey, then wiped them on the last clean rag she had. "He'll be hurting for a while, but no major blood vessels were damaged. His sternum caught two of the shots and one slug was stuck between two ribs. He was lucky that Wilson had a light load in his bullets."

"Yeah, well, that might not be a coincidence," Branson said, grinning sheepishly. "Just don't tell anyone — especially Wilson. I think more than one person is alive today because I'm the one who reloads his bullets."

"Who is he?" Mary asked Branson as she tidied up. "I've never seen him around."

"He's just a gambler who came into town, I suppose. Seemed a decent sort, but he knew what he was doing when it came to cards. I don't know his name, so I guess it's a good thing he didn't die. We don't need another unknown drifter buried on Boot Hill."

"He told me his name," Petey said. "I remember 'cause it's kinda like mine. He's Peter Wagner."

Mary's hand froze on her medical bag. "What?" she asked and spun around.

"Peter Wagner. Not Petey, but close."

She quickly threw the curtain open to let in the first rays of daylight. "Hand me that lantern," she said, reaching toward Branson.

"Yes, ma'am," he said, handing it to her. "Is there something wrong?"

Mary held the light close to the wounded man's face with one hand, pushing his dark hair from his forehead with the other. "No. Not wrong," she said and took a deep breath to compose herself. "I thought he was dead."

"No, Mama. You do good work. I don't think he's gonna die now. He just needs rest."

Mary looked up at Branson, then turned to her son. "Petey. He's your father. That's why your names are the same."

"But you said my father died before I was born," Petey said. He stared wordlessly into the man's face, studying his features, wondering if this was what he was going to look like when he grew up. "You said he was going to live, right?" he asked.

Mary chuckled. "You're the one who said he was going to live, but yes; I think he's going to live. That is, if he keeps away from Banker Wilson and his gang of thieves."

Branson cleared his throat. "You'd better watch what you say, too." He glanced over at Petey, still intent on studying his father's features, one finger tracing his eyebrow. "I really don't think Wilson cares if he hurts a woman. He's wanted this place for a while. It's the last house on the street that's not his. But regardless, I'd better get back to the saloon. I was just supposed to be dragging his carcass to his horse and then sending the two of them on their way. Petey talked me into bringing him here. Kinda hard to say no to him, ain't it?"

"Yeah," Mary said, looking at her son, worry skewing the features on his young face. "It is."

***

"What took you so long?" Wilson asked Branson when he walked in the back door. "I give you a job that shouldn't have taken an hour, and you come traipsing back when it's almost noon."

"Hey," Branson said, his lack of sleep causing him to speak fearlessly, "What I do in my off-hours and who I happen to spend time with is my own business."

Wilson, took a deep breath, his hand floating up to his gun.

The bartender saw the gesture and changed attitudes. "A man has needs, you know," he said, then cupped his privates through his pants. "And sometimes it takes a little longer than others," ending the comment with a wink and a sly grin.

Wilson's hand returned to his side. He shook his head and smiled. "You devil you. I thought you lost the urge after your wife died last year."

Branson snorted. "Like I said, sometimes it takes longer than others. Some ladies like it like that. Now, if you don't have something else you want me to do, I need to make sure the shelves are stocked for tonight, and then I want to take a nap. That woman took a lot out of me!"

"Who...?" Wilson began, then stopped

as Branson shook his head.

"I don't share," the wily bartender said. "Even her husband leaves her alone."

"Well, as long as it isn't my wife, we'll get along fine."

Chapter 2

The next day

"Would you like a drink?" Petey asked when he saw his father's eyelids flutter.

"Where am I?"

Petey grinned so wide, he thought his bottom lip would split. "You're at my house, Pa."

Peter groaned, sure that he was dead or having visions because he was so near it. He shut his eyes again, and heard his angel singing her favorite hymn, 'Rock of Ages.' "Mary. Marry me, Mary," he said softly, then drifted off again.

"What are you doing, Petey. You let that man rest," Mary scolded as she dried her hand on her apron.

"But Ma, he was waking up. I told him where he was, and that he was my Pa, but he just went back to sleep. Do you think that something happened to his hearing? Maybe he didn't hear me right."

Mary looked down at the sweet face that she had been in love with since she was twelve. As soon as they were old enough to marry, he disappeared. Her father told her that he'd been killed in a logging accident. She leaned in close and brushed the hair from his forehead and saw it in the bright morning light. An old jagged scar. She did some quick math in her head. Yes, it had probably happened six years ago.

"You weren't killed!" she exclaimed in a harsh whisper.

"No, but I think death would be a might less painful," Peter groaned, his eyes now squeezed tight. "Where am I and is my mare all right?"

"You're here with me, Peter. In the home your grandmother gave to us as a wedding present," Mary said, hiccupping her words as happiness and grief struggled for dominance. "You're alive!" she squealed, then bent forward and kissed him hard on the mouth.

"Whoa! What?" Peter stammered, still confused about where he was and why this woman was kissing him. He tried to lift his head, but stopped at the pain. "Ah, jeez!"

"Oh, I'm sorry," Mary said, urging him to lie back down. "I had to cut three slugs out of your chest. It's gonna hurt for quite a while, but give it time, and you'll be as good as new." She giggled. "No, better than new since I thought you were dead. You're alive!" she squealed again.

"Yeah, I kinda got that impression, hurting and all," Peter rambled, his fingers twisting the coarse bedsheet between his fingers. "'cause, once you're dead, the pain is gone."

And then he was out again.

"Did you tell him where he was?" Petey asked, peeking in from the parlor.

"Yes, dear, but he didn't understand.

I'm sure he'll be better in a day or two. Why don't you take this and run into town and buy some meat? He's gonna need some hearty beef broth to get his strength back. Cabbage soup won't do it."

Petey pushed the coin back into his mother's palm. "I'll use my money," he said. "The money my pa gave me before he knew who I was." He smiled broadly. "Jeez! I liked him even before I knew he was my pa."

"Thanks for the help. And you're right. He was always a good man." She sighed deeply. "And now he's back."

***

Petey pushed the door halfway open and looked inside.

"I thought I told you to keep outta here!"

"I got money today, Sir. My ma asked me…"

The storekeeper saw the banker walking up, and dragged the boy aside. "Get outta the way! I got a real customer." Patting the wrinkles out of his apron and dripping with nervous sweat, he pasted on a phony smile and said, "Hello, Mr. Wilson. What can I do for you?"

"You can hang this up where folks can see it," and handed him a sheet of paper. "The bank was robbed last night. That gambler that was passin' through did it, then skedaddled. Sheriff won't be back for a week yet, so I'm putting together a posse. We'll get him taken care of right away," he said and tilted his head, miming a hanged man.

Petey's head went from one man to the other, his teeth clenched tight in anger. He knew not to speak up — he'd made that mistake before — but Mr. Wilson was boldface lying. Mr. Branson had told him that it was the banker who had shot his pa. There was no way he could have robbed a bank; he was still in bed and couldn't even walk. He'd bet his one and only coin that Mr. Wilson robbed his own bank. He ground his teeth, trying to keep the growl silent. First, the banker tries to keep his mother from making a living with the boarding house she owned outright, then he shoots his pa. Now he was trying to pin a bank robbery on him, too. Someone needed to do something about that horrible man.

"What are you doing in here?" Banker Wilson asked Petey. "Looking to buy a new pair of shoes?" he asked, looking down at Petey's rag-tied feet, laughing boisterously.

"No, Sir," Petey said, teeth still clenched. "I'm buying a beef roast for Christmas dinner. I heard some folks get to acting extra nice at this time of year. I was hoping to get one big enough for a few meals for me and Ma. How about it? Do you have the Christmas spirit of giving yet?" Petey asked, mimicking the words the pastor had used the week before.

"Oh, why not, Henry," Mr. Wilson said. "It's not as if you'll go broke giving folks their whole dime's worth. Give the kid a break. Can't you see he needs a little meat on his bones?"

The shopkeeper swallowed his grumble, then went in the back to take a small roast out of the icebox. "It's still cold, but you'd better have your ma cook it right away." He sniffed it and wrinkled his nose. "Good enough for your kind."

"Now, get outta here, kid," the banker said, shoving the boy through the doorway. "You're letting in the cold air."

"But," Petey started to protest, then realized he had both the roast and his coin. "Merry Christmas to you, too," he shouted back, then sprinted toward home with his prize.

"Whoa, there, lad," the sheriff said, reining in his horse at the near collision. "What's your hurry?"

"Sheriff Behan!" Petey shouted, then looked around, making sure the banker and grocer were still inside the store. "Could we talk? In private?"

The sheriff chuckled at the small boy who seemed to have serious business to conduct. He nodded towards the alleyway and walked his horse toward it. "Now, how can I help you, son?".

"Mr. Wilson thinks you won't be back for a week. He's putting together a posse to lynch the guy who robbed his bank, only it wasn't really robbed. At least, not by the man they put on the wanted poster. That man was shot by Mr. Wilson hisself. My ma's been tending to him for the last day and a half. He's at our place right now. You could see for yourself his condition."

Sheriff Behan adjusted himself in the saddle as he thought about it. Yes, it was cold and he wanted to get home right away, but if this was a chance to nab Wilson, he'd take it. "Come on up here and ride with me. We'll get to your place faster on horseback."

Three minutes later, Mary greeted the pair at the door, a wide smile on her face at seeing her son had hitched a ride back with the sheriff. "Good afternoon, Sir," she said.

"Ma!" Petey screamed, then slipped off the saddle. He gave her a big hug, then whispered, "I didn't tell him he was my pa," then pulled back and declared, "Mr. Wilson is saying the man you fixed up robbed his bank last night. I brought the sheriff here so he could see that he wasn't in any shape to do it."

"Come on in," Mary said, accepting the paper-wrapped roast from her son. She sniffed it. "Looks like it's a good thing I have lots of onions and pepper to add to the pot."

"Well, I'll be," Sheriff Behan said when

he saw the familiar face. Peter was propped up with pillows, sipping a hot brew with his one functioning arm, his chest wrapped with yards of linen strips, a bright red shawl draped across his shoulders. "If it isn't little Petey Wagner, all grown up."

"Hey, Johnny," Peter said. "I didn't know you were in this part of the world." He noticed the star on his chest, "And the sheriff, to boot?"

"Yeah, I'm the sheriff. This boy tells me that Lee Wilson's telling everyone you robbed the bank last night. Looks to me like you either got shot doing it or Wilson's trying to put one over on the townsfolk again."

Peter set his cup down and snorted in disbelief as he tried to sit up straighter. Mary saw his dilemma and was at his side, urging his shoulders forward as she repositioned the pillows. "That pork-bellied, card-switching thief is the one who shot me!"

"Yeah," Petey interjected. "And the bartender saw the whole thing. He even brought my pa here yesterday so my ma could fix him up. He was shot three times, weren't you, Pa?"

"Pa?" the sheriff asked. "He's your son?" He looked from one to the other and said. "Yup. No denying he's yours. Not that I wouldn't claim this one. He's a sharp kid."

"Yeah, well, if I'd known Mary was here, I would have tracked her down. I was told that she ran off with some salesman after she found out I'd been hurt in a logging accident. I figured she must've fallen for the guy pretty hard."

"You're the one I fell for pretty hard," Mary said. "And even though my father insisted you were dead and I should marry someone else, I couldn't do it. I still had the deed to this place. When I found out I was pregnant, I decided to make a new, fresh life for me and our son. There's no way I was gonna marry that old mill owner my father had picked out for me."

Peter's eyes opened wide. "So, that explains a lot. The accident wasn't an accident: it was attempted murder. Someone was trying to get me out of the way so he could marry you."

"Well, folks, I'd love to stay and catch up on old times, but looks like I need to see if I can catch old Mr. Wilson red-handed."

"I'd offer to help, but…" Peter said.

"Don't worry about it. Wilson doesn't even know I'm back in town. Plus, he's got a new girlfriend his wife doesn't know about. Two to one that he's hiding the cash there. Let's see if I can make this a quick day."

Chapter 3

"Hiding something or just discovering it?" the sheriff called out.

"Who? What? Why are you here?" Wilson asked, quickly putting something behind his back. "And what are you doing in my house?"

Sheriff Behan tipped the brim of his hat up with the barrel of his gun. "Well, for one, I'm here investigating a theft. And for the other, this isn't your house, it's my cousin's."

"Why'd you let him in, Sharon?" Wilson huffed, then dropped the saddlebag he'd been stuffing with cash and deeds to the floor. "I should tan your hide for that!"

"You'll never lay a hand on me ever again," Sharon said, then flipped back her hair to reveal the black eye. She turned to the sheriff. "Yes, Johnny. This is the man who robbed his own bank. He said he was going to Bisbee and sell the deeds, then take all the money and sail to Alaska and mine for gold. I told him I didn't want to leave, so he hit me. Bad mistake, Lee."

"Anything else you want to tell me?" the sheriff asked her.

"Other than he hides his aces in his vest pocket, underneath his handkerchief and is a lousy lover, no."

The sheriff stepped between the banker as he lunged at his former girlfriend. "Not in the Christmas spirit, eh,

Wilson? Come on, I'm taking you in. Whether you're sitting in the saddle or draped over it is your decision."

***

"Elph?" Peter asked. "How'd you come up with that name?"

Mary blushed. "I would have used your name, but that wouldn't have been right since we weren't legally married. When Petey was born, the midwife said he looked like a little elf; cute and tiny with little ears poking out. So that was it. Peter Elph. When we moved here, I took his name."

"I see. So, Mary, will you marry me, even if I can't get down on my knee to ask?"

Giggling, Mary squealed in excitement, her hands clutched under her chin, "Yes!" She calmed down and bent to kiss him. "Did you know this is about the tenth time you've asked me in two days? You kept asking in your delirium."

She bent to kiss him, tentative and cautious of his wounds. "It's a good thing we already had the honeymoon. Looks like it might be a while before you're healthy enough for your husbandly duties."

"Don't worry, my sweet Mary. Let's start with the kissing, then work up to building a little sister for Petey."

Just as their lips touched, Petey burst into the room. "It's time! Sweet Mary is having her baby!"

Peter struggled to get out of bed, his grunts and groans of pain escaping clenched jaws.

"Back in bed, Peter Wagner," Mary said. "You have a wife and son to help you now. Petey's assisted in birthing cats, dogs, goats, and cows, so he should be ready to help me pull a foal."

***

Christmas morning

"Wow!" Petey exclaimed. "Where did you get this? I've always wanted one." He handed the carved horse to his mother.

"It really is beautiful," she said, winking at her new husband. "Your father has many talents. Creating works of art from firewood is one of them. This is almost as beautiful as Little Leopard."

"I'm still working on the name. The colt's half Arabian, so maybe The Sheik of Arizona," Peter said. "Either way, with his lineage, he's more valuable than fifty mining claims."

"Hey!" Petey exclaimed. "I got it! How about Silver, like his color?"

"Hi-ho, Silver!" Peter called out and chuckled. "Yup. Sounds pretty good to me. Silver it is."

***

And they all lived happily ever after.

***

The End

Afterword

Thank you so much for reading **Peter Elph**, part of **Christmas Shorts**. If you would, please take a moment to leave a review for this story and/or the box set on Amazon or Goodreads. Your insights help other readers decide if a book is a good fit for them. It also gives the authors the feedback they need/thrive on. Thanks!

Contact information:

Email: dani@danihaviland.com
Twitter: @dani_haviland

I love to hear from readers!
Sign up for my newsletter to get the latest information on new releases, free stuff, and contests at: http://bit.ly/2DHnews

Awesome readers make up a street team!
I have a Facebook Page for folks who are interested in early excerpts and insights into my latest books and box sets. I'd appreciate a like on the page. Drop in and see if I've remembered to add photos and excerpts of my works in process. http://bit.ly/2DaniStTeam

About the Author

USA Today bestselling author and entrepreneur Dani Haviland started writing late in life and has been making up for lost time with a torrential flood of romances. Savor them all but start now. More are coming, and you don't want to get too far behind!